TENNESSEE
TIGER

TENNESSEE TIGER

J. L. Küntz

Illustrated by
Tina Wells Davenport

Scythe Publications, Inc.
A Division of Winston-Derek Publishers Group, Inc.

© 1996 by Scythe Publications, Inc.
        A Division of Winston-Derek Publishers Group, Inc.

First printing

PUBLISHED BY SCYTHE PUBLICATIONS, INC.
Nashville, Tennessee 37205

Library of Congress Catalog Card No: 93-60259
ISBN: 1-55523-611-1

Printed in the United States of America

To Norma Love Whitehead-Küntz,
for steadfastness beyond Motherhood

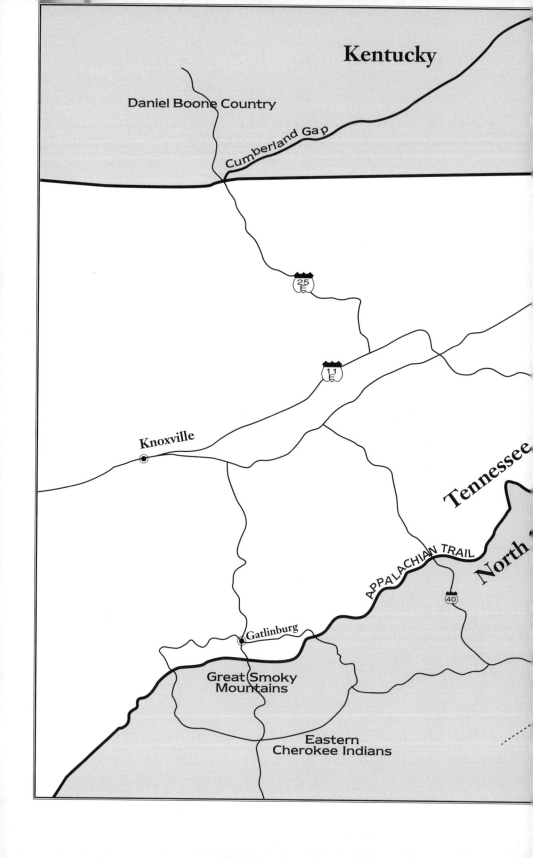

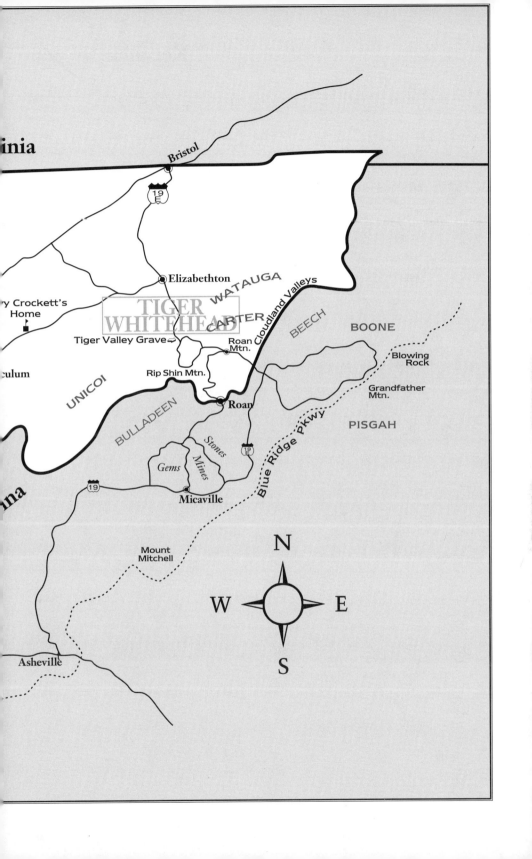

Contents

In the Tiger's Den

Thor Whitehead was worried. It was late morning, and his older brother and sister were at middle school. His mom was at a Sierra Club meeting to keep the mountains and rivers clean, and his dad, the park ranger, was at work at Roan Mountain State Park, making sure no one cut the laurel bushes or picked any of the wild plants and herbs. There was no one at home this morning except Thor and his grandmother. But she was too old to protect him from tigers!

Thor sneaked outside to the rocky stream that ran through their mountain farm. He saw his metal Space Invaders stuck in the sand. He was scared, and he wondered if he should go back inside and load his father's rifle—the one that had the big hammer on it and had belonged to Grandpap Whitehead. Standing up beside the big rock where his brother and the big boys went diving in the summer, Thor realized that little boys couldn't pour powder into guns that were like bean poles and taller than they were. He could perhaps ask his grandmother. But no, she had told him never to play with his grandfather's rifle. So he put his hands in the cold spring water, feeling hot tears in his eyes. Why did there have to be tigers in Tennessee, anyhow?

Thor's dad had told him there were bears up on Rip Shin Mountain, and grazing deer with big antlers on White Rock Mountain, and wild pigs with foaming teeth on Buck Mountain. Worse yet, there were wild Indians who had black bears for pets in the Smoky Mountains! Still, Thor was not too upset, because his dad said that they were far, far away.

Today the world was a cloudy place. For a moment, Thor listened to the rushing stream and watched the white water come down the small brook and foam over the flat rocks. He turned back toward his house and saw that his grandmother was sweeping the front porch. Unsure of what to do next, he built himself a little boat out of sticks. He glanced back to the porch, where his grandmother stood watching for him. She called, "James Thor Whitehead!" He didn't answer.

After a few moments, she picked up her broom and went inside. Before she could come back out onto the porch, Thor took the secret path around the big rock to the clubhouse.

Back under a ledge, the fire Josh had built last night was completely out. Thor poked at the soggy charcoal. Josh had covered it with ashes the night before—that was how the Indians had kept embers hot. Thor had wanted to take some of the dry sticks and get the fire going again so he could hide under the rock and not get wet. The little fire would keep him warm, and the tigers would be afraid to come near it. But now everything was dripping.

He couldn't hear his grandmother calling for him anymore, so he backed under the ledge and listened to the rain. The harder it rained, the faster the little brook ran over the rocks.

Suddenly, he thought he spotted something moving up the stream, among the rocks. Then he shivered, remembering that Josh had once called the stream "Upper Tiger Creek." Thor looked upstream, but the ledge blocked his view, and it was so misty that he couldn't make out what or who the intruder was. It seemed to be working its way around some rocks to get closer to where he was. Maybe the tiger used this ledge for its home when the big boys were

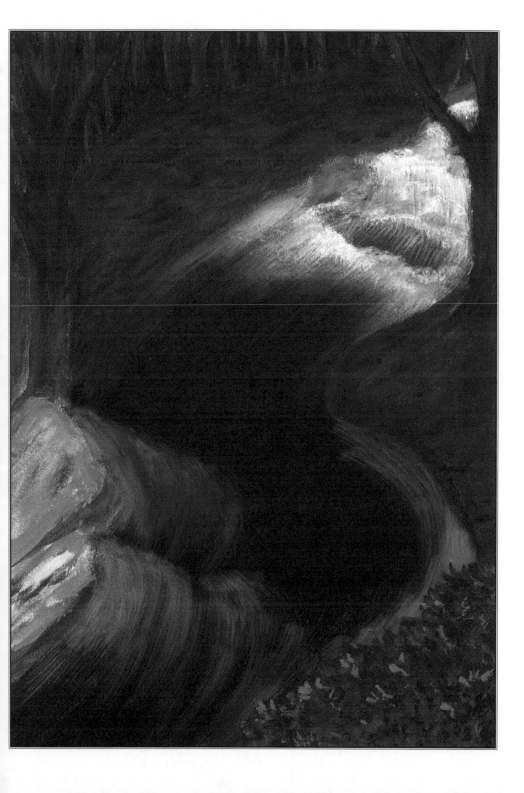

at school! Thor knelt down to the soggy fire and frantically dug out the wet ashes, looking for a hot coal. He found one, but it gave no more than a spark when he put a dry leaf on it and blew his hardest. But he kept at it, and soon the leaf began to burn. Without looking, he quickly scooped up a handful of leaves and dumped them on the tiny fire. His heart sank when he realized too late that they were wet, and the small flame vanished with a puff of smoke. How could he make a mistake like that? Where was his brother Josh when he needed him?

Thor knew that Billy Bobcat lived in the deep ravine on the other side of the stream. His dad had taken him out one night last week to listen to Billy growling in the dark. Hearing the animal's wild cries, Thor had imagined just how long Billy Bobcat's teeth were. But weren't tigers bigger than bobcats? His sister had said so. What would happen to him if the tiger upstream got between him and the secret path back to his house? How would he ever escape? Suddenly Thor feared that he must be in the tiger's den! And he didn't want to be eaten alive!

Upper Tiger Creek

Despite the amount of rain they'd gotten recently, the stream didn't look all that deep. Thor had seen it worse. He wasn't going to stay here and face Mr. Tiger—not in his den. Everyone knows that a little boy is no match for a tiger, especially a Tennessee mountain tiger. Thor had on his old work boots, but he was also wearing his good coat. He knew his grandmother would be mad if he got it wet, but he also knew that he heard something move behind the rocks, prowling the wet bushes. He could wait no longer. He went upstream as far as he could, because the water was too deep below the ledge. Thor knew there was one place where the stream was swift but shallow, and he decided to cross at that point. Mr. Tiger would never follow him now!

For Good Friday, the creek was still cold. The white dogwoods hadn't bloomed yet, and the potatoes were unplanted. As a matter of fact, Good Friday was the day his family usually planted the early crop of red potatoes, branch lettuce, and green onions. With his face staring down into his reflection, Thor edged out onto a flat rock that sloped down into the swirling water. But once he felt the cold sting on his warm feet, he knew he was in trouble. Then he slipped, and the creek was up to his knees. There was a black root that lay out like a rope on the other side. He tried to take a giant step and reach it, but the swift water caught his boot, and he went down into the white swirl.

At first Thor thought he was in a dark, cold tunnel. He held his breath, just as his brother had taught him. He turned over and over until he bumped up against a big rock. Without mercy, the water swept him down again, past the ledge. His small body tumbled over a waterfall, and at last he came to rest in a shallow, sandy pool. He feared that he would lie there dazed until he died.

After a few moments, Thor realized that the pool was only knee deep. He frantically crawled out of the creek and scrambled up a bank. He stood up, trembling. At first the trees and the swift stream were spinning all around him. The mountains and his house had no real place. When he finally got his bearings, Thor realized that he was on the wrong side of the stream, looking back. He gazed up the stream, past the ledge to the rocks, where he again saw something moving. It darted back and forth, this time in plain sight. Thor felt sheepish when he realized that it wasn't Mr. Tiger after all. It was Mrs. Opossum looking for her breakfast among the roots and vines. The soaked little boy watched her waddle down to the slippery rock, sniff two or three times, and turn back for the protection of the ledge. Heck! He had let a 'possum scare him.

Dazed, Thor sat down. He stared across at the opposite side. No! He was not going to try and cross the stream again. His grandmother would tell his father that he had been playing in the creek. Thor had stayed home from school today because he was sick with the flu. And Dad would want to know—if Thor was so sick—why he was playing outside in the rain. That meant there would be no surprise tomorrow—or probably ever! Tomorrow was Saturday, and Dad had promised him something very special bright and early. They were going on a trip to meet an uncle who was a very famous hunter.

Cold and shivering, Thor decided he should try to get back home as soon as possible. With his cold fingers, he felt underneath his

tightly buttoned coat and realized that his undershirt had not gotten wet. He would just have to brave the elements like his father said all hunters have to do from time to time. But the big question was how he was going to get back in time. Maybe his grandmother wouldn't miss him. She was getting old, and she didn't remember like she used to. But from where he stood, Thor could see her up on the porch, looking around the yard for him. She had that look about her that spelled trouble. He would hurry home and hopefully lessen the pain of punishment.

Thor began running, and he could feel the cold water dripping down his legs. Ahead was a wide path that traveled downstream and led right by old Mr. Crawford's house, where a bridge crossed the creek. Thor didn't want to go by Crawford's place, but there was no other way to get back. He had only seen Mr. Crawford once, but he had heard all the stories about him—about how mean he was, especially to kids! Still, it was only late morning. Maybe the old billygoat slept until the afternoon, before he started guarding his bridge.

It was a long way to Mr. Crawford's, and Thor ran harder, dodging the rain-laden vines and weeds that flanked the path. He was already thinking about how to sneak around Mr. Crawford. Josh's friend Zeke had told Thor that the old man kidnapped kids and used them to grind up stones. All the kids said that Mr. Crawford knew how to take ugly rocks and turn them into diamonds and jewels. He sold them in Knoxville and brought back silver bars for his big black safe. He was supposed to be the richest man in the mountains, even though he lived like an old grizzled billygoat.

The path now slipped into a dark hollow. Thor had been on this side only once, last winter when the creek was frozen over with ice. But he had never been down this far before. In the tree branches above him, the heavy vines closed in and blocked out the daylight. As the path grew darker, sharp needles of cold water bit into his legs, and his eyes darted from side to side. For the second time that day, James Thor felt like he was in a tunnel.

Mr. Owl, Johnny, and Boots

"Whooo, whooo...whooo..." asked Mr. Hoot Owl, "is watching you?"

Thor stopped abruptly. He stood frozen in his tracks. "I guess I'm watching myself," he replied softly, looking around for the source of the voice.

Perched upon a dead tree limb, a grizzled old owl shut his left eye. "Doo...ooo your mom and dad know that you are watching yourself?"

Thor stood quietly in the darkness. "No, I guess not," he admitted. "But...but the tigers are after me, and I have to get back home!"

A big drop of rain fell from the dead tree onto the owl's head, causing the big, placid bird to stretch its feathered neck. Now he shut his right eye. What a silly excuse for being lost, Mr. Owl thought to himself. I haven't seen a tiger here since the hunter left. "Well, little boy," the Owl said aloud, "parents are always worrying."

Thor gazed up through the trees at the dark sky. Mr. Owl, who expected a response, shut both eyes this time. "My mom's at a meeting," Thor mumbled. "She'll be back at noon."

"Pfffh! Run along, little boy," Mr. Owl grumbled. "Mr. Crawford keeps a fire blazing while he grinds his stones. I have mice to catch. In this land, we are all hunters. Don't look so scared, or you might get eaten by this tiger you are talking about!"

Thor walked on. Passing a heavy clump of bushes, he stepped into a small ravine that was even darker than the path had been. Feeling all alone, he turned around to see if Mr. Owl was still there. But all he could see were the high green leaves and branches weighed down with rain droplets that looked like silver diamonds.

Slowly he stepped deeper into the ravine. He still couldn't see Mr. Crawford's house. He thought he should have come upon it by now. Maybe he should turn back. His feet didn't want to go anywhere, and the cold was making his legs numb.

If he had not been such a brave hunter, Thor would've started crying right then and there. But he wisely realized that he was not alone. He could find whatever friends he needed.

"What are you doing here?" he asked out loud.

A frightened squeak came from inside a nearby laurel thicket. "I'm hiding from Mr. Owl," said a little field mouse. "I know he's watching me, but I don't know where he is."

"Shhhh!" Thor whispered. "Mr. Owl will hear you. Here, jump into my coat pocket, and you can go with me to Mr. Crawford's."

The field mouse climbed up onto Thor's wet clothes, and the boy placed him gently inside his right coat pocket. "By the way," whispered the little mouse. "My name is Johnny."

"Nice to meet you, Johnny. I'm Thor." Before he started off again, he turned around, expecting to find Mr. Owl right behind him. Whew! Mr. Owl was nowhere to be seen. So Thor hurried on through the ravine with Johnny the field mouse scurrying around in his pocket.

Presently, they came upon a small stream of water rushing down from the steep sides of the newly green mountain. It cut directly across their path. But this one was a little kid stream, the kind that even Thor could jump over. At a narrow point, he steadied his shivering legs and poised himself for the leap. But a squeaky voice came up to him from the cold, dew-laden ground.

"What are you trying to do," demanded a little box turtle, "step on me—break my shell? It's the only home I have!"

Thor paused, startled. "Oh, no," he said, looking down. "I'm sorry. I didn't see you." He turned so that Johnny could see, too. "Here, look! It's a little turtle."

The field mouse stuck his head out. "It is, it is!" Johnny said. "I've never seen a turtle that small before."

"My name is Boots, if you don't mind," said the turtle, relieved that he hadn't been stepped on.

"Hey, Boots!" the field mouse yelled. He looked up at Thor. "I used to have a brother named Boots, until that craggy old owl got him. What are you doing away from home on this rainy day?" he asked, addressing Boots once again.

The little turtle looked down. "I went out looking for my mother," he cried. "I thought she was gathering food by the creek. But when I got there, she was gone. Now I'm lost and can't cross the stream."

Saddened, Thor bent down and said, "Here, climb up into my other pocket. We're going to Mr. Crawford's, so I can get home. Don't feel bad. I'm sort of lost, too."

"Yeah," Johnny said. "Come along with us. I always wanted to meet a box turtle."

Now that he had two traveling companions, Thor didn't feel so lonely. The dark tunnel of trees he had been passing through for the last few minutes was beginning to thin out, and the cold suddenly didn't sting so bad. He thought that he wouldn't mind at all if Johnny and Boots became his very own pets once he got home. But he would have to wait and see. He was not going to take them away from their homes and families if they didn't want to come with him.

Making sure they were safely secured in his pockets, Thor leaped across the little rushing stream, then hurried for Mr. Crawford's house without really knowing the way.

Miles To Go Before I Sleep...

Presently, it began to rain again, and Thor started to worry. He knew that his grandmother would be very upset with him. Somehow, he had to get back before his father found out he was gone.

To Thor's dismay, the path led him into the darkest part of the ravine once more. He wondered why he had never seen these hidden valleys before. His father had told him last winter that the land across the creek was a wilderness, and no one but Mr. Crawford lived there. And where was Mr. Crawford's house, anyway? Worse yet, what if he wasn't home?

Just before it stopped raining, Thor emerged into a small, green field that was used to pasture the sheep and newborn lambs. It was the most peaceful sight he had ever seen. The gently rounded field continued up one side of a steep green hill, and on the other side stood a large barn where a dozen shaggy ewes guarded their baby lambs. Thor wondered if he should go over and get warm in the hay with them.

"Hey kid," Johnny the field mouse said, whistling through his teeth. "You don't need to go over there. Believe me!"

"Why not?" Thor demanded.

"Because the mothers are still in mourning," Johnny answered. Then he saw Thor's confused look. "Look," he explained, "some of the lambs died because it got too cold this spring. And you wouldn't want to see me cry, would you? I get very emotional." The field mouse waited for Thor to say something. "The ground froze thirty-nine inches deep this winter. My family and I had to live in a snake hole!"

"Yeah," Boots cried. "I wasn't even born yet. But my mom said she almost froze to death herself."

Thor stared across the field at the sheep huddled together, next to a huge haystack by the barn. He wished his mom was with him. "But I feel so sleepy," he said. "Couldn't we just go over and get warm?" He turned and looked back at the dark ravine they had just come from. It didn't offer any comfort, either. "I can't fight my way out," he yawned. "The sleep monster won't leave me alone."

"Hey, Thor," Johnny whistled. "Remember me and Boots! We all have a long way to go before we can sleep. Mr. Owl will surely get us if we stop now. If I gotta die, I want it to be at least sixty degrees above freezing, in some place nice and sunny!"

Thor thought about Johnny and Boots. They trusted him, and he didn't want anything to hurt them.

"Okay," Thor said, "we'll round the field and head back towards the creek. Mr. Crawford's place has got to be over there."

To stay warm, Thor ran as fast as he could. After all, he had to think not only of himself, but of Johnny and Boots as well. He couldn't give in to the sleep monster right now. He had to hurry and cross that mountain, then he had to sneak past the old billygoat who guarded the bridge to freedom and home.

Soon Thor came upon more trees as he moved away from the green pasture. Glory! There was the rushing creek. "Look, Boots!" Johnny shouted. "We've found the stream!"

Boots peeked out of Thor's pocket. "Let's run as fast as we can," he said, his voice as soft as flying milkweed. "I'm afraid of billygoats. I'm just a baby turtle, remember."

17

Thor had strong legs, and they were running as fast as an Indian's painted pony. Boots and Johnny had to hold on tight just to keep from bouncing out of Thor's coat.

"I can see Mr. Crawford's house!" Thor shouted. "That's got to be it. And look! There's smoke coming from that chimney."

"Oh boy!" said Johnny, his little black nose poking out from the pocket. "Don't worry, Boots," he whistled. "Thor's not scared of billy-goats."

"I'm so glad you found me," Boots said. "I would never have gotten home again."

Johnny was whistling as loud as he could. "Me too! Who needs some big old owl hovering over you all the time?"

Looking for Mr. Billygoat's House

All Thor could think about was the fire inside Mr. Crawford's house. Maybe the old man was gone on one of his trips. They could sneak inside, get warm, and hurry home before Thor's father found out.

No one was in sight at Mr. Crawford's, but the chimney was boiling with blue smoke. Thor tried the house first. In every room there was enough furniture for a dozen people. He even looked in a bedroom. But no Mr. Crawford. Finally, he decided to look in a small, neat cabin that stood directly behind the yellow-white, two story house. He had to be very quiet, because he remembered that Mr. Crawford had a dog or cat or something. So he tiptoed up to the side porch and eased over to a window.

With his small fingers, he wiped the moisture and grit from a window pane until he had made a small, round hole. Through it he saw a large fireplace made out of river rock directly across from the window. The fire was so hot that he could feel its warmth on his cold, red face and fingers when he touched the glass. The orange-red flames suddenly roared up from the cut logs, and Thor felt a chill run through him. The walking and running had kept him warm, had

kept his blood moving. But standing still with the cold wind blowing behind him made him feel like his wet clothes were biting into his numb body. Thor didn't want to go home with his clothes dripping wet, and he certainly didn't want to freeze to death along the way. Surely Mr. Crawford wasn't as mean as all the kids said he was; surely he would let Thor warm up by the fire.

Thor cleaned off some more of the dirty glass. The wooden-floored room was stacked full with boxes of rocks and stones. Some were royal blue, emerald green, or orange-yellow; others were rough and muddy brown. Then he caught sight of Mr. Crawford's solitary frame bent over a high work bench, where a small motor turned a silver drum. Mr. Crawford watched the whirling drum intently for a moment, then flicked a switch with his gnarled fingers. The drum stopped spinning, and he opened it up. Taking a handful of stones from the drum, he held them up to the light, examining them closely. In a matter of seconds, the rainbow of colored gems was back in the drum, and the motor sounded again.

Thor glanced across the cluttered bench. At one end, perched upon a bookcase filled with large books, was a huge black and grey cat. It mirrored every movement that Mr. Crawford made by flipping its long tail back and forth like the pendulum in a clock. One moment the cat was watching Mr. Crawford, and the next its green eyes focused directly on Thor. It let out a low, grumbling "Meeoow!"

"That cat's talking to the old man," Thor whispered.

"What?" yelled Johnny the field mouse. "Cats?!"

When the old man rose, turned, and limped to the door, Thor knew he had been discovered. He suddenly panicked. Now he was trapped! It was raining so hard that he couldn't see beyond the edge of the woods. By degrees, the wooden door slowly opened, and Thor tried to hide behind a large wooden barrel.

"Little boy," Mr. Crawford called, looking around. "Little boy!"

Thor's heart pounded violently. He turned sideways to avoid squashing Boots or Johnny.

"Socrates, did you see that little boy?"

21

"Meeoow!"

"Where did he go?"

The gigantic cat walked squarely through the door. Trying to stay hidden behind the barrel, Thor listened to the heavy raindrops hit the tin roof. After a couple more meows, Socrates leaped up onto the top of the barrel and stared down at him. All Thor could see were two big, marble-green eyes. They blinked, and Thor could have sworn that they changed color to blue.

"Little boy," the old man said gruffly. "Little boy! Come out from behind that barrel. I know you're back there."

Thor slowly stood up, stumbled from behind the barrel, and faced a rather small, bent-framed man. Upon seeing Thor's red face and big eyes, Mr. Crawford pushed his goggles to the top of his head and crossed his arms in front of him. "Now where's your friends?" he demanded. "I'll have no rock throwing at my house today. No tricks!"

Thor didn't know what he was talking about. Perched upon the barrel, the cat craned its head up and down. Thor could feel Boots and Johnny scurrying around in his pockets. He knew they felt trapped and were afraid that they were about to be discovered, too.

"Well?" Mr. Crawford demanded.

Thor didn't know what to say. He couldn't throw many rocks over twenty feet—and never at someone's house.

Socrates and Mr. Crawford were waiting. Thor was so cold he wondered why he didn't have icicles hanging off of his burning ears. Dismayed, he knew there was no way to win. He either froze to death or was eaten alive by a billygoat all because he wanted to cross his bridge. "I got lost," Thor blurted. "I live up the creek. I fell in, and I came here to get dry. There's no way to get back across, except use your bridge," he finished, pointing around the front of the house.

Mr. Crawford came closer. He touched Thor's jacket. "Why, Socrates," he exclaimed. "His jacket feels like ice."

"Meeoow!"

"The fire and a cup of coffee will take care of that," Mr. Crawford said. "Here, come inside my gem shop."

23

Socrates Sees Polaris

Thor and his hidden guests followed Mr. Crawford and Socrates back into the cabin. The big black and grey cat instantly sprang back up to the top of the dusty bookcase, leaping as if his rounded body could fly.

Mr. Crawford put a high-backed chair in front of the hearth. "I have some good hickory firewood," he said. "It will dry you out fast. Put your coat on the back of this chair."

"Meeoow!"

"I'm surprised you didn't freeze to death," Mr. Crawford said, arranging the coat so it hung down freely. "Socrates here has been with me ever since my wife died," he explained. "I can't hear very well anymore, so he meows every time I don't hear something."

To Thor's cold, numb body, the hot flames were soothing. He knew that Boots and Johnny must be enjoying the fireplace too, because steam began to rise from his coat.

"I think my coat is getting hot," Thor said. "Let me move the chair back some."

Mr. Crawford grinned. "I told you that hickory wood got hot."

Thor sat back down and looked around the room. He was amazed at the array of rocks that Mr. Crawford kept in his cabin. "What do you use all these rocks for?" he asked.

"Rocks! These aren't *rocks*—they're precious stones and gems."

Everywhere Thor looked there were boxes of rough rocks and stones, in all shapes and sizes. Some were in piles, others were still in their crates. And some had been cracked open. Thor could see where the chips had fallen. "Do you collect rocks?" he asked.

"Here, have some of this coffee," Mr. Crawford said, smiling. "Sometimes. I'm really a gemologist. I make rings and bracelets. See?"

Amazed, Thor stepped over to a glass case, sipping the heavy, dark coffee, getting a mouthful of chicory. Inside were rings, bracelets, and trinkets of all sizes. He especially liked the aqua blues and ruby reds.

"All my life I wanted to collect gems," Mr. Crawford explained. "Now I go to digs in North Carolina and prospect for them." He pushed his goggles further back on his head. "Which reminds me, you ever think about being a pebble pup?"

Thor looked first at Mr. Crawford, then over at Socrates. "Digs? What's a pebble pup?"

"Digs are big sand pits the size of football fields. And a pebble pup is another name for a rockhound, someone who goes around digging for precious stones—only younger."

"Wow!" Thor couldn't imagine a sand box that large. It sounded like fun.

Mr. Crawford took a stone from the metal drum on the work bench and held it up to the light. "I'm polishing stones at the moment. See how rough they are? I put them in here, and the sand inside polishes them." The old man returned the stone to the drum and flipped the switch on. A small electric motor began to hum. Socrates focused intently on Mr. Crawford and the drum.

Slowly, Thor moved his chair closer to the fire. Then he stood between the chair and the hot fireplace. It wasn't long before he could feel the warmth radiating through his body. The tops of his jacket's

pockets were open, and he could see the little field mouse pointing at Socrates. Even Boots was trying to get Thor's attention.

"Meeeow!"

Mr. Crawford turned the motor off once again. He opened the metal drum, took out four stones, and examined them through his thick goggles. Meanwhile, Thor had turned around to dry out the front side of his clothes. The heat and light felt so good that he shuddered.

"See this one?" the old man asked, holding the stone up to the light. "Polaris! The God of Light and Resurrection. Reach for a star, Socrates."

"What is it?" Thor asked excitedly. "Does God live in Polaris?"

"Depends on your faith, my good boy." Mr. Crawford eyed Socrates. "Now, as I was about to say, this one is the earth's sun. A yellow sapphire," he began, his admiration of the stone's inner qualities very evident. His gnarled fingers held out the plum-sized rock. "I'm going to take this one to Knoxville. I know it doesn't look like much right now, but there's a prize inside it. I'll cut it in two, then I'll polish her up until she sparkles in the dark.

"Ah, hush up, Socrates. I know, I know, it's the star...a miracle!"

"Why, is it worth a lot of gold, Socrates?" Thor asked.

"Meeow, meeow!"

"Some," Mr. Crawford smiled. He took a piece of blue cloth and began shining the stone's yellow surface, gazing over at the cat's shining green eyes.

Still admiring the sapphire's beauty, he quietly said, "You haven't told me how you got so wet."

"Meeow!"

Billy Bobcat and the Tennessee Tiger

James Thor Whitehead thought for a long moment. This was one time he did not know what to say. He was ashamed to tell Mr. Crawford and Socrates that he had been playing behind the big rock and let a 'possum scare him so badly that he very nearly drowned in the creek. Thor knew his Space Invaders would never have been scared like that. They would have investigated and found out the truth.

So Thor waited until he could look Mr. Crawford square in the eye. "My brother told me about this bobcat that lived across the creek—you know, Billy Bobcat, the one that has big teeth and makes the growling noises at night?"

Mr. Crawford stared straight at him, unbelieving. Socrates just said "Meeow!" Both were thinking, what an imagination he has!

The little boy was somewhat tongue-tied at first. His dad would call what he was about to tell Mr. Crawford and Socrates a tall tale. Meeting Mr. Crawford's piercing eyes, Thor knew he had to make his tall tale good.

"I first began to construct a bridge made out of river rock," he explained. "I had my dad's hunting knife, and I was going to look for bear like Davy Crockett. My brother and I have been listening for Billy Bobcat every night this week. I figured out where Billy was going to be this morning."

Mr. Crawford shut the drum off. "What happened?"

"Meeow!"

"What happened? Uh—" Thor hadn't constructed this part of the tale yet. "I...I was carrying this big stone to the top of the bridge I made, and I slipped and fell in. And it washed me up on this side of the creek."

Mr. Crawford started laughing. "Sounds as if you're a first-class hunter to me." He took the blue cloth and wiped dust from the stones. Thor drank the last of the hot, bitter coffee. "See how they begin to sparkle?" Mr. Crawford asked him.

Thor took the bluish stone and saw that it was studded with specks of purple and black. It was really beautiful. He wondered how much gold it was worth. "Mr. Crawford, I've been meaning to ask you, how do stones get blue? I, um," Thor said, taking in a deep breath, "also want to know about this big tiger that roams these mountains."

"What tiger?"

"You know. He's the one I really want. After I get Billy Bobcat, I'm going after him. Tigers and bobcats shouldn't be allowed to roam around scaring people!"

Mr. Crawford laid out the seven stones, one by one, on the wooden table. "Meeow!"

"Okay, Socrates, I'll put the ruby last. What do you think?" he asked Thor.

"They're really pretty!"

Mr. Crawford got up and threw a large log on the dying fire. As if by magic, new orange flames erupted. He then sat down, facing the red-faced boy, who obviously needed someone to straighten out this fabricated tale about tigers in Tennessee.

"About a hundred years or so ago," Mr. Crawford said smoothly, taking off his goggles, "there was this gigantic, striped tiger that

30

roamed the bald peaks, green mountains, and rocky tops. Some say he traveled as far south as the Unicoi Range, and as far north as the Virginia Blue Ridge. But Carter County, Roan Mountain, and Whitehead Hill were primarily his home. And it's rumored that he killed ninety-nine bears."

"Boy, that's a lot of bears!" Thor cried. "No wonder they call this Tiger Valley." Thor knew he'd be late getting home now. But surely his mom and dad would understand that he'd wanted to hear this story. But why hadn't they ever told him that this tiger had killed ninety-nine bears? Just like Space Invaders, he must have been some wild catasaurus!

"Meeow! Meeow! Meeow!" Socrates was swishing his tail as if thoroughly troubled by the conversation.

"I know, Socrates. I'll tell the tale as true as my father and grandfather told me," he said. He glared at Socrates as if he were agitated. "My father and grandfather used to tell me about the tiger. My father said he even caught a glimpse of him once, up on White Rock Mountain. But he hid in a thicket of mountain laurel, and then they couldn't find him. Right before his death, my grandfather used to tell me that the tiger had the ability to disappear when humans tried to capture him."

"You mean he could vanish into thin air?" Thor asked.

"Yep! He could go into these laurel thickets and then just be gone. The Cherokee Indians, before they left these parts, used to wear laurel leaves with their feathers as a sign of bravery and immortality."

Thor looked up at the smoky ceiling. It had stopped raining. The tin roof was no longer pounding with the spring downpour.

"What ever happened to this tiger?" Thor asked, realizing that this must be the tiger that his brother was always talking about.

Mr. Crawford gazed at Thor with a blank grin on his face and blinked his watery blue eyes. "No one really knows," he answered. "They say that his descendants roam the mountains and creeks from time to time. But I'm sure the big tiger is gone now. Maybe he's gone to the Smoky Mountains to kill bears with the Cherokees!"

"Is that the reason they call this place Tiger Creek?" Thor asked.

"Yep! So you see, Thor, you live in a famous place. It's one of the last free places in this country. It has wild streams, wild mountains, and little boys like you to play in them."

"Meeow!"

"I guess you're right," Thor answered. He could hear Johnny scurrying around in his coat. The hot fire had heated his clothes up, and he knew that his little friends must be getting toasty warm. He looked from Mr. Crawford to Socrates, to the fireplace, to an unmoving cuckoo clock that was mounted above the work bench. He only hoped that his grandmother had not called his father.

"Well," he said. "I guess I must be going. My clothes have dried out some. Someday I'd like to come back and be a pebble pup—maybe this summer."

Mr. Crawford was all smiles at the prospect of getting such a fine young helper. "You know, Thor," he said. "You've been a bright light in my day. I don't get many of those any more, since my wife died. We all like a little light once in a while."

Mr. Crawford took a small aqua-green stone from his blue cloth. For good luck, he rubbed it a couple of times. "Here, take this with you," he said. "It will protect you from the tigers. And come down and see me sometime. Just think of all the stones we could find together. My big black safe couldn't handle all the gold we'd make!"

Thor's eyes lit up as he took the small gem. He held it up to the light, watching it sparkle and dance. Then he slid it into his shirt pocket, next to his heart.

"Thanks," Thor said. "Now I owe you something."

"Meeow!"

"Don't worry about it," Mr. Crawford replied. "Only the tiger will ever know."

The Bridge Back Home

Outside, the grey clouds hung low over the steep sides of the placid mountains. Fortunately, it had stopped raining. Thor hurried down the rocky lane leading to the bridge that would cross the creek and take him back home. He hoped that his grandmother was napping or had taken something for her asthma.

Johnny the field mouse stuck his head out of Thor's coat. "Hey, Thor," he called. "What took you so long? I was getting hot next to that fire!"

"I know, I know," he answered. "I'm sorry about that."

"Yeah," Boots said. "But it was a lot nicer than being cold."

"At least that big monster Socrates didn't find us," Johnny added. "That was some mousetrap—'meow, meow, meow!'"

"Okay, guys," Thor said. "Here's the plan. We'll sneak home, and I'll get you some food. My grandmother will be taking her nap by then. You can sleep in my room tonight."

Thor rounded a bend in Mr. Crawford's gravelled lane that was heavy with trees, plants, and bushes. Up ahead must be the bridge. In fact, he thought he could see some wooden planks in the distance. If

he ran, he could be at his house in a matter of minutes. Soon, this misadventure would all be over!

Rounding the bend, Thor came to an abrupt stop as he reached the first timber. He could feel his heart in his stomach. Below, the waters from the muddy creek roared past the swollen banks. And on the other side of the bridge in a group that stretched across the road were his mom, his dad, his grandmother, the next-door neighbors, and his black labrador puppy, Sinbad. All waiting for him.

After a moment of silence, Sinbad started barking wildly. Thor knew he was in trouble. They would never believe his tiger story now. But it was too late to do anything except face them.

For the longest time, all Thor could hear was the rushing creek. Behind his parents, the green mountains jutted steeply toward the sky, and a herd of cattle grazed at an angle. Time seemed frozen. Thor felt like he would either pass out or turn and run back toward the dark ravine.

First, his dad frowned severely at him, then he silently motioned for Thor to come closer. His dad and the threat of punishment scared Thor the most, but little by little, he heard the planks echo under his wet boots as he crossed the bridge. Finally, his mother grabbed him, squeezing him tightly.

"James Thor, we were so worried about you!" she said, her eyes brimming with tears. "Where in the world have you been?"

"Tigers, Mom, tigers," Thor blurted. "They were after me. Even Mr. Crawford knows about tigers. Someone should have told me."

Thor's dad and grandmother laughed.

"I don't know how you can find this so funny!" Thor's mom cried. "Two years ago, when you had to go into the hospital, that's all you talked about! Tiger this, and tiger that. It was like your family was the only one around here that had any heritage!" She started crying. "See, this is all your fault."

Thor's dad looked dejected. "I know. I know. And I said that I was sorry about all that. Dr. Cooper told us it would be painful for Thor this way. But it will be best for all of us in the long run."

"I hope you're right," Thor's mom said. "We need to put an end to this tiger myth!"

Thor's dad bent down in front of him. "Well, Thor, after tomorrow, you won't ever have to worry about tigers again," he said, smiling.

"Really? No more tigers? Did you hear that, Johnny and Boots?"

With two small hands that were cold and red, the smiling boy pulled his friends from his pockets. "See, Mom? This is Johnny the field mouse and Boots the box turtle."

"I guess they go with Sinbad the sailor dog," she said, beginning to smile, too.

"Where did you find them?" his grandmother asked. "Before long there won't be enough room for all of them."

"Johnny was hiding from an owl," he answered, excitement showing in his face. "And Boots was trying to find his mother. They had no place to go. I'm going to let them stay with me for a couple of days." Thor held the two animals up for everyone to see. Then he carefully placed them back in their hideouts.

"And look! Mr. Crawford gave me a good luck stone."

His mother and grandmother moved closer, anxious to see if the old goat had given the little boy anything of value.

"Hmmh!" his grandmother snorted. "Mr. Crawford must have liked you."

"Why, Thor," his mother gasped. "It really is beautiful."

"See, I told you that he gave me a good luck stone!"

"Quite a stone for quite a young man," she replied.

He started shivering. "Mom, I'm cold."

"Your dad has gone to get the truck," she said. "We're going to get you home and put you into a nice, warm bed."

Thor's grandmother took her coat off and draped it around his shoulders. It was heavy and hung down to his boots. "Your dad has talked so much about tigers this week," his grandmother began, "I guess your imagination got carried away. Son, it's not good to go around chasing after tigers. One of them might turn around and eat you!"

38

As Thor listened to his grandmother, he gazed up to the steep, velvet-green pasture and the high, windblown trees on the ridge behind the road. Just for a fleeting moment, he thought that he saw the big tiger running on a mountain trail under the trees on the ridge line. A shiver ran up and down his spine, and his heart soared. But as quickly as he had spied them, the tiger's stripes vanished into the mist.

Mommy on the Duck Pond

Thor's dad brought their large four-wheel-drive truck rattling down the road to where they were all standing, and Thor, his family, and some of the neighbors got in for the short drive back to Thor's big white house. It was there that the search for him was called off. Afterward, the cold and tired boy spent the rest of the day tucked under a pile of quilts and blankets while Boots and Johnny played in their nearby cages.

All afternoon Thor kept wondering when his dad was going to be angry with him. He feared him so much that he almost felt like he was in a cage like Johnny and Boots. Thor could remember very well when his dad had nearly lost his job and their house two years ago. At that time, there'd been periods of open hostility between his mom and dad, and the whole family had finally had to move out to his grandmother's house. It had gotten much worse when his father went away unexpectedly one day. There had been no goodbyes, no explanations. The hardest thing of all was listening to his mother cry at night in his grandmother's bedroom.

In the end, it was his grandmother who held them together. Thor still remembered her long speeches on "the serpent drink," as she called it, and the sickness of practically every man that she had ever known—even her own son. Like the rest of the family, Thor's grandmother found occasion to blame herself for the problems and heartache that her son caused his family, and she had done her best to help them all get through that dark time in their lives.

Thor had found it especially difficult to understand what was happening. He just couldn't figure out why they wouldn't let him visit his dad at the hospital in North Carolina. In fact, Thor hadn't really understood why his father had to go away.

Late one afternoon back when the mystery of his father's absence had been especially confusing and frightening, Thor's grandmother had told him a story in the hopes of making him feel better. Thor had been all red-faced and teary, and he'd started to cry once more. "Mommy on the duck pond!" his grandmother had announced. "Look, Thor! Look at me!"

She bounced him playfully on her lap as she began her story. "There is a beautiful, crystal-clear pond, way up on top of Rip Shin Mountain," she said, her voice soothing him. Then she peered down into his dark brown eyes with a glint of mischief in her own. "There were two ducks that lived on this looking-glass pond, back under tall hemlock pines beside a thicket of laurel bushes. The mommy duck was a smartly-painted brown, and the father duck was a handsome mallard, with the most gorgeous green head in all of creation. Why, when the sun shone through the pines and laurel bushes, it was as if God had created a rainbow."

"Was he green like my turtle that just ran away?" Thor asked.

"Yes. But of course, it was a finer, more velvety green, like my dress."

Thor nodded his head as he looked up at his grandmother, his eyes wide. "Oh!"

"But underneath the sparkling surface—beyond the mirror—all was not well in the pond."

"No?"

"No! There were two tribes of fish that lived in this pond," she informed him. "The rainbow trout and the horny head fish."

"Horny head fish," Thor repeated. "I don't like the horny head fish!"

"I know you don't."

"The horny head fish has little horns on it that cut you when you try to get them off your hook."

His grandmother smiled. "Well, the rainbow trout family that lived in this sparkling pond lived lives of luxury and excess. They had everything they could want: food, a nice cave under a mossy rock to live in, and plenty of time to swim from pond to pond, waterfall to waterfall. And of course, they are the most beautiful fish in all the rivers and streams.

"The horny head family, on the other hand, were a lot different. They had to eat periwinkles and dead worms to survive. And their home was an old hollowed-out log. Worst of all, they are the ugliest of all fish—why, sometimes they are scorned by everyone that they live with."

"Kind of like the rock man, Mr. Billygoat!" Thor suggested.

"Why, yes, Thor. But even he has a good place in his heart." This surprised Thor, because his brother Josh had always told him differently.

"Well, among these two tribes of fish in the pond, there lived a handsome young rainbow trout and a wild young buck from the horny head family. The trout was named Beauty Boy, and the young buck was called Little Bump.

"As was very likely in the small pond, they met each other one day, when Beauty Boy saw Little Bump trying to leap the falls that led upstream beyond the Duck Pond. Because he was so small and ugly, the young, sleek trout swam over to the falls, laughing. 'What are you trying to do?' Beauty Boy asked. 'Why, hasn't anyone ever told you that the horny head fish can't jump? They make their living lying on the bottom, as scavengers.'

"The little horny head fish didn't know what to say. He had heard that there was more food to eat just above the falls. And he thought that maybe he could find his family a new home under a mossy bank, if only he could jump the falls.

"'I can jump as high as you can,' Little Bump stormed.

"The beautiful, speckled trout started laughing again. 'Well, let's see it,' said Beauty Boy.

"Still angry, the horny head fish backed up, and—swimming his hardest—aimed for the very center of the falls. Arching his body, he leaped upwards into the foaming falls, cleared the rushing water, and for a moment was flying in the bright sunlight. But his little body was so small that the rushing water pulled him back down into the Duck Pond. But this defeat didn't stop Little Bump. He tried again, and again, and still again, until he was exhausted and too tired to even talk.

"The trout swam over after watching these attempts and said, 'See my tail, see how it's made? You need a tail just like mine. Watch.' Little Bump watched the trout bolt for the falls, leap, and sail through the air. Then he was gone—into the next pond.

"After the trout disappeared, Little Bump felt saddened. Everyone in his family had said he couldn't fly, and sure enough, they were right.

"So the little brown fish decided he would swim home, but he wouldn't tell anyone that he had tried to jump the falls. But he knew—deep in his heart—that he would give just about anything to find out the secret of jumping the falls. Little Bump had convinced himself that magic must be involved. The whole world must be magic, he thought, if a certain few could do what others could not.

"Back home, no one in his family mentioned his absence. And boy, was he glad! He was so afraid that his mom would ask him where he had been. But everything was quiet. Even his grandmother did not question his absence.

"The next day, Little Bump waited for his family to begin their daily chores. Once his dad and his brothers and sisters were gone,

Little Bump told his mom he was going out to play with Squeaky the blue gill fish. Instead, he swam along the dark bank, by the trout's home, and headed straight for the falls.

"But when Little Bump got to the falls, much to his dismay, no one was there. Little Bump swam all over looking for Beauty Boy, the handsome trout. He even swam through the rushing foam that the falls make, looking for the magic secret."

"What did Little Bump do, Grandmom?" Thor asked.

"Why, he devised a plan," his grandmother answered. "He decided that he would try to jump the falls until Beauty Boy or one of his friends showed up.

"So Little Bump began swimming and leaping, swimming and leaping—leaping through the air. Once, he almost made it! Then, around noon, Beauty Boy swam up, laughed, and said, 'I see you're still trying to do the impossible. But I don't blame you. There is plenty to eat and drink just beyond the falls. It's a paradise up there.'

"Hearing this made Little Bump want to fly over the falls even more than before. But since he already knew that he couldn't fly like the rainbow trout, he realized that he must discover the magic secret—even if it meant doing something his family would not approve of.

"'Tell you what I'll do,' Little Bump said to the Trout, who was swimming around him in beautiful circles.

"At first, the sleek trout swam by Little Bump, pretending not to hear. Shortly, though, he swam close and said, 'What's that, Little Bump? Do you want me to make you a new tail?'

"'No,' replied Little Bump. 'But if you teach me how to fly over the falls, I will give you half of everything that I claim for myself.'

"The rainbow trout grinned. 'I will make you a better deal than that. If you give me half of everything, I will show you where the magic door is that leads up under the rocks and comes out above the falls!'

"'Magic door!' Little Bump exclaimed. 'I knew there had to be a secret path somewhere!'"

Thor's grandmother suddenly grew very serious and somber. "Beauty Boy was actually being dishonest and evil with Little Bump," she said. "The magic passage was a place that was only spoken of in ritual services, and it was only used when an evil fish had died and was taken there for burial. It was a place, Thor, where relatives could pray for the cleansing of the sins of their loved ones. Beauty Boy's father had told him to never, never use it, because he feared that no one could return from the sacred grave of the dead. But being the unruly little trout that he was, Beauty Boy thought that this was some superstition his father might have made up. That's why he decided to send the ugly horny head fish into the sacred passage. If Little Bump came back, Beauty Boy would know for certain that his father's story was false!

"Upon hearing mention of the secret passage, Little Bump was so excited, he couldn't stand it. 'Where is it? Where is it?' he asked Beauty Boy. 'I want to see what the next pond looks like!'

"Beauty Boy, seeing Little Bump's enthusiasm, set aside the forbidden oath he had made to his father and grandfather. Besides, that had been a long, long time ago, and Beauty Boy could always say that the oath had slipped his mind.

"'First off,' Beauty Boy said, 'you must promise me that you will never tell anyone what I am about to show you; and second, you must mark the secret passage at the top with a periwinkle, so you will know where to enter on your way back.'

"'Beauty Boy,' Little Bump replied, 'I will promise you anything to find out where the magic door is.'

"Hearing this, the trout smiled. 'Okay, follow me very closely, because we're going into the falls where the maze of bubbles is so thick, you can't see! You must use your fins to touch the rocks, and use the faint green places of moss as a guide. My dad says they are Holy!'

"'What, Beauty Boy? I didn't hear you.'

"'It was nothing, Little Bump. Just stay close to the green moss.'

"So Beauty Boy swam off, very slowly, and Little Bump followed. After only a short distance, the roar of the falls was so great that Little

Bump almost lost Beauty Boy. But the little fish hung in there and stayed so close he could feel the trout's tail swishing his nose. Together, they crept along the base of the mossy rock, but in the next instant the thunder of white water swept them clear across the pond to the other side. When the current subsided, Beauty Boy and Little Bump found themselves under a muddy bank, drifting calmly downstream.

"'I have forgotten the way,' Beauty Boy said, flaring his gills because he was out of breath. 'It's a killer under those falls!'

"'I know,' breathed Little Bump. 'I almost lost you.'

"For the first time, Beauty Boy looked at Little Bump and saw not an ugly brown horny head fish, but someone who was a lot like himself.

"'Listen, Little Bump,' Beauty Boy said. 'Are you sure you want to do this?'

"Little Bump thought and thought and thought. 'I can't jump the falls like you,' he finally said. 'Please show me the magic door. I'm not afraid!'

"'Okay. But we need to start from the other side and stay closer to the base of the falls. I hope I can find it.'

"This time, Beauty Boy and Little Bump circled the pond, swimming as close to the base of the rock as they could. Beauty Boy had to stop several times and touch the green, velvety moss on the rock, using it as a guide. Once, they were nearly swept out, but they hung on to the curtain of green. At last, they came to a cleft in the rock that abruptly turned back to the left, and Beauty Boy danced around excitedly. 'This is it, this is it! I know it is. The cleft rock!'

"Little Bump's heart beat wildly. Everything his family had always wanted and dreamed of would now come true. He swam alongside Beauty Boy once the waters had calmed.

"'There it is,' Beauty Boy said, stopping, suddenly afraid.

"'There's what?' Little Bump asked.

"'The mirror.' Beauty Boy sounded frightened.

"The reflection from the mirror was so bright, it appeared to be on fire. And behind that loomed a darkness that Beauty Boy could

feel from the depths of his soul. Again, Beauty Boy wanted to ask, even plead with Little Bump not to go into the secret passage, or through the magic door. But Little Bump was beside himself with excitement. He swam up to the mirror and touched its glowing glimmer. He even stood half in and half out of its fiery veil.

"'I will make you rich for this!' Little Bump exclaimed. 'Half of everything I find will be yours. Neither of us will ever grow old or be hungry again.'

"'Little Bump, it's dark in there,' Beauty Boy called. 'Maybe you shouldn't go.'

"Little Bump was dancing in the veil. 'Don't be silly. I will be back before you know it.' Little Bump waved a fin to his new-found friend, Beauty Boy. Then he disappeared into the fiery glow.

"At first, the way wasn't dark, and Little Bump was not afraid. For a moment, he stopped and stared back at the veil, a shiver of excitement running up and down his spine. Very clearly, as if through a window, he could see Beauty Boy still swimming there, waving his fins frantically. Outside, Beauty Boy was afraid that Little Bump had already gone too far. But inside the passage, Little Bump had no way of knowing what Beauty Boy was worried about. Little Bump only wished that Beauty Boy had come with him. After all, they were friends now. But of course, Beauty Boy could jump the falls on his own. He didn't have to use magic!

"Little Bump had always been told never to be afraid of the dark, because there was a guardian spirit that watched over little horny head fish and kept them safe. But as he tried not to fear the darkness, he also worried a little about his family. He had not told his grandmother where he was going or what he was trying to do. He knew that his grandmother would never have approved of his deal with Beauty Boy, nor would she have ever approved of Little Bump using the magic door.

"But Little Bump didn't have time to worry; he needed to be brave! So, puffing up his gills as big as he could, Little Bump swam on into the blue-black tunnel that only gave a faint hint of light at its

51

end. Swimming hard, Little Bump became aware of the dark tunnels that branched off to the right and left. Slowing down, he let his curiosity get the better of his judgment. Feeling adventurous, Little Bump swam into one of the dark caverns. But just as quick as he swam in, he shot out, his heart racing! The cavern was full of the bones of dead fish, all arranged in rows. And some looked as if they had recently died!

"With his fish scales standing on end, Little Bump eased his way further down the dark tunnel, wondering if he would have to swim through this every time he wanted to get to the upper falls. Was this some kind of cemetery? It was getting kind of spooky, and he wondered if he should turn around and go home. But he trusted in his family's belief that a spirit would follow him in times of need, so he swam on. The tunnel never seemed to end. All along the way, Little Bump saw where new tunnels had been carved into the rock. Each one, he presumed, was filled with the skeletons of dead fish. When Little Bump's heart was finally about to cry out from fear of the unknown, the passage began to head up a steep incline. Even better, he could now hear the falls roaring ahead. Suddenly, Little Bump came out into a room filled with lights that sparkled and drifted down from above. It was so bright that he could not see for a few moments after the darkness of the passage. Intensely frightened, he covered his eyes with his fins and stopped swimming. But he didn't want his fear to overcome him, so he slowly opened his eyes and saw a huge altar surrounded by gold. Behind that was a shimmering bright light.

"'Maybe this is the upper pond,' Little Bump thought. But then he realized that there were still rocks over his head, except at the far end where the sun dazzled through the crystal clear water. When he realized he was seeing daylight, he was flooded with relief. Surely that was the entrance to the upper pond!

"Excited, Little Bump swam around, spinning triumphantly on his tail. His family would never be without anything! Without hesitation, Little Bump dashed over to the altar and touched its gilded top.

Instantly, his fin and the whole right side of his body were stung by an electric shock that knocked him backwards towards the blackness of the passage!

"When he came to, he was trembling. Trying once more to swim for the light, the little brown fish grazed one of the golden rocks. Again, he was shocked and lost all control over his movements! Panicking and flapping his little fins, Little Bump struggled for the open hole. This must be some kind of test, he thought. To see if I deserve the freedom of the upper pond.

"Finally passing through the light, Little Bump entered a cavern. This one was larger than the last. Up ahead he could see a shimmering light like the one at the entrance that Beauty Boy had shown him. 'Ahhh!' he breathed. He knew that freedom was moments away.

"Like Jonah in the whale's belly reaching for the hand of salvation, Little Bump reached for the fiery veil. He floated closer and closer, and still closer. He was swimming with all his strength. Then he hit it. Shhhhhzzzzz! Instead of going through it, an electric shock hit him with such force that he was paralyzed. For a few minutes, he couldn't move. His whole body hurt, even the little horns on his head. The room grew dark and hazy, and Little Bump thought he must be dying!

"By this time, all Little Bump wanted was to get out of there. He knew something was wrong. He should have told his grandmother where he was going. She would have said that nothing is worth the risk of using magic.

"When he finally awoke, the little horny head fish was floating upside-down. He had drifted down into the cold, dark tunnel, slightly below the steep incline. He immediately wanted to get out of there, because now it was freezing. It might be night for all he knew, and his family would be searching for him. Unfortunately, he was still paralyzed. Worse yet, he feared he would float into one of the caverns where he had seen all the dead fish.

"Little Bump waited for what was actually minutes but seemed like hours. He had visions of fish eyes staring at him from the dark

54

caverns, where he floated by, unable to do more than raise a fin. Voices from the spirit world began to talk to him. And then suddenly and terribly, he thought that he must be in hell!

"Little Bump began to weep at this realization, not for himself, but for his family. In the darkness, he longed for his family and began to see how foolish his adventure had been. Without ever realizing it, he had risked everything for nothing. Now Little Bump would have only his death to show for it. The secret passage—the magic door— had obviously been a trick. He should have practiced harder and then jumped the falls instead of looking for the easy solution. But now it was too late; he had defied the sacred laws of the spirit world!"

Thor's grandmother was suddenly quiet. She sat very still, rubbing Thor's back. She was proud of her mountain story.

Her grandson sat upright. "Grandmom!" he cried. "Did Little Bump die in the tunnel?"

"No, Thor," she replied. "The caverns were actually part of a great temple, and after Little Bump came to, a spirit from the temple came and saved him. But because he had trespassed on sacred ground, he was never permitted to leave the burial caverns or the temple. And he could only see his family from behind the fiery veil. Yes, he could talk to them, but he could never touch them. And a long, long, long time after this happened, Little Bump grew to become an old fish and was the wisest, most revered fish of the spirit world. He was the only fish on Duck Pond to ever have the power of the spirit world and still be part of this earth! He was the only horny head fish to ever become a prophet." Grandmother paused once more, breathing deeply.

Thor, still saddened by the story, wanted to hear more. "Grandmom, what happened to Beauty Boy?"

Suddenly troubled, his grandmother stared at him. "James Thor, it was awful," she began. "When Beauty Boy's family found out what had happened to Little Bump, they rushed to the falls and the fiery veil. The rainbow trout grandfathers and grandmothers sobbed as if judgment day had arrived. They couldn't believe what Beauty Boy had done, especially since he violated the family's code. All the rainbow trout were afraid that their own spirits, and those of the fish who had already died, had forever been violated. For them, the temple was the first step on the way to paradise. And knowing the secret to the magic passage was one thing that made a rainbow trout special. Shamed, the rainbow trout felt that Beauty Boy had ruined the spiritual part of their lives.

"But the shame did not stop there," Thor's grandmother continued. "Because Beauty Boy was so scared and so sorry for his trickery, he ran off and hid among the horny head fish. He rolled himself in mud and leaves and tried to cover his beautiful spots.

"Meanwhile, the rainbow trout family cried rivers and rivers of tears for losing such a beautiful son. It was decided that all rainbow trout fish had to do something for the horny head family, to pay for Beauty Boy's sin and deception and for the fact that he had desecrated the secret passage.

"So they all held an assembly of each tribe's grandfathers and decided that the two fish families should from then on live together in peace—that they would share food, homes, and each others' happiness as well as misery. So the bright spots began to mingle with the muddy brown skins as both tribes worked to clean out a new place under the mossy bank by the laurel bushes where the horny head fish could live. It wasn't long before they each realized that the other had skills and ideas that everyone could use.

"Of course, that didn't help the rainbow trout family cope with the loss of their son. They knew that fate would not shine favorably on him because of his sin. In time, Beauty Boy lost his beautiful spots and became as brown and nondescript as the horny head fish. And this is how it happened:

"Beauty Boy was swimming one day out on the far end of the pond, rolling in the muddy bottom. It was a sunny day, and the water was crystal clear. One moment he was frolicking on the muddy bottom, and the next he looked up through the pure, clear water and saw the face of a gorgeous tiger! Being something of a tracker himself,

Beauty Boy thought that the tiger was after him and would eat him for food. He knew that this was the end he deserved: to be killed and eaten. But the tiger left him alone. This strange event scared Beauty Boy so badly that he stayed in darkness for days. Afterward, he decided to live in the very same hollow log that Little Bump's family had once occupied. Through the long, cold winter under the ice, Beauty Boy's spots began to fade, and one day he woke up and was as brown as the muddy bottom!

"Having lost the one thing that he valued the most—his beauty—Beauty Boy was never the same. It's rumored that after one or two attempts to see his cousins, he ended up marrying a horny head girl and raising a family of horny head fish."

On that afternoon, two years ago, when his grandmother's tale had ended, Thor had sat still, thinking. Then he had asked, "Grand-mom, is everything all right on the Duck Pond now?"

"Yes, Thor," she had answered softly. "Everything is all right on the Duck Pond. The people of Tiger Valley come and go between the deep, blue gorges of Rip Shin Mountain and Bulladeen. The lily pads float endlessly by on the placid waters as the thick ferns sway in the cool summer air. And the mommy duck takes her family for walks up through the laurel bushes toward the Roan, and the beautiful, velvety green papa duck sparkles in the pond's everlasting sunlight!"

Thor and Sinbad See Their Star!

Lying in his bed, half hidden in the warm blankets, listening to the little field mouse playing in its cage, Thor said to himself, "I guess the tigers do come out at night!" He sighed, wondering if his dad would make good on his promise, even after everything that had happened.

In any event, he still had his two little friends and a good luck stone to be proud of. Thor waited until everything was quiet in the house and the only sound to be heard was the wind coming up the valley on its way to Rip Shin Mountain. The little field mouse had stopped playing on his wheel, and Boots was resting on a rock in his aquarium. Quietly, Thor slipped out of the warm blankets and knelt beside his bed. A shaft of bright moonlight peeked in from behind the curtains.

"Dear God, please bless Mommy and Grandmom White-head. Bless my dad, and help him stay out of the hospital. Take care of the family, and thank you for sending me Boots and Johnny. And please bless Mr. Crawford and Socrates for helping me out today. Oh, yeah—please bless my dog Sinbad for taking care of me. You and he were the only ones that knew where I was! Amen."

A wet, cold nose tickled Thor on the back of his neck, under his hair. "Oh no, oh no," he giggled. "I love you, Sinbad." The big black puppy, his auburn eyes the color of fire, licked the boy's face. "How did you know I was awake? Huh?" Thor buried his face in the dog's neck. "You knew I was gone this morning, didn't you?" Sinbad cocked his head sideways and stared at him. "Hey, Sinbad, you want to go look at the stars?" Thor could hear Sinbad panting in the darkness.

Together, they went to the window and pulled the curtains back. Sinbad jumped up and placed his front paws on the window sill and leaned up against his master. Thor couldn't believe how bright the full moon was. It shone through the dark blue night and highlighted the ridges and trees. The stars dotted the sky like thousands of silver-painted Christmas lights.

"Look, Sinbad, there they are. See?" The dog licked him in answer. "Dad says that direction is the north. And see the one that's just off from the Dipper? That's our special star. That's where we'll go some day! You'll chase birds, and I'll kill tigers!"

Sinbad couldn't believe what he was hearing. He loved to chase ducks and geese! Thor closed the curtains and called softly to Sinbad. The dog trotted over to the bed and, reaching the far corner, curled up in his spot. Thor slipped under the heavy quilts once again, feeling Sinbad lying on his feet like a warm rock.

Channel Three's News Truck

The next morning dawned clear and cold, and the clouds and mist had been replaced by a fierce open sky. While it was still quite dark, Thor's father came in to wake him up. "James Thor Whitehead," he said, throwing the blankets back. "We've got to hurry. We can't be late!"

Upon realizing what his dad was talking about, Thor was so excited that he forgot about how much trouble he'd been in the day before. Feeling as if a giant weight had been lifted from his shoulders, he quickly washed his face, brushed his teeth, and dressed in wool clothes.

His mom and grandmother were waiting in the kitchen. There was just enough time for a glass of cold juice and a bowl of steaming oatmeal. Thor couldn't help but notice that his grandmother seemed the most pleased of everybody. For her it was "ol' John L. Whitehead coming back to life," the hunters going to the fields with the dogs.

"Well, son," Thor's dad said, drinking the last of his coffee. "It's time to take care of that tiger."

"What is it? Where are we going?" Thor asked excitedly.

"In good time," his father answered, then smiled. "You'll see. And it's something that you will never forget!"

Together, father and son hurried to the big truck. Sinbad was waiting and climbed into the truck with them, barking. Thor's dad started the engine, and they quickly headed down the glistening black road.

Thor sat back in the seat, wide-eyed. With the sun just crossing the mountains, everything seemed so much different. Even the Jersey cows high up on the mountainsides, still hidden in the early morning shadows, seemed to sparkle. Beyond Mr. Crawford's house, the sheep were huddled next to their haystacks, eating. Their breath looked like little puffs of smoke. Things far away seemed close, alive!

"Look, Dad," Thor said, pointing. "Mr. Crawford is up, too. There's a big fire in the fireplace."

"He's probably grinding gems," Dad replied.

It wasn't a long drive down Rip Shin Road. They passed the newly plowed gardens, white houses, and checkerboard farms, until they came to a conglomeration of people and vehicles parked all around the quiet country road. Thor knew that they had stopped just up the road from where Tiger Creek met Tiger Valley.

"Hey, Dad!" Thor shouted. "It's Channel Three's news truck!" Everywhere he looked, men were carrying lights and electrical equipment onto a path that led up the side of one of the steep, rounded mountains.

After they had parked, Thor first wanted to see the cameramen doing their jobs. He ran up to the large news truck that had pulled off the side of the road and waited for the door to open. Above him, two men climbed on top of the truck to arrange the antennas. The large van had almost as many gadgets as Thor's Space Invaders. Even Sinbad was excited at what was taking place.

"Son," his dad called. "Come over here. I want you to meet someone."

Thor was so excited, he couldn't believe all this was happening. His fear of tigers was a million miles away.

64

"Thor," his dad said, "this is Mr. Robert Bragg. He works for a newspaper in Chattanooga."

A big, bearded man in a wool suit and hat stuck out his massive hand for Thor to shake. He had a pen and pad under his left arm. "Is this the son you were telling me about?" Mr. Bragg asked.

"He sure is," his dad answered. "Thor was named after his great-great-great-uncle, James T. Whitehead. His brother Josh wanted his middle name to be Thor."

"And he's Tiger Whitehead's youngest living relative, as far as you know?" Mr. Bragg asked, writing on the pad.

"Yes, he is," Thor's dad replied, smiling at his son. "My grandfather was seven when Tiger died in 1905 and only remembered him from his childhood. Our family still has what mountain people call the 'hog rifle' that was used to kill the majority of the ninety-nine bears. The rifle was given to me by my grandfather, just before he died."

Thor watched the reporter take down every word that his father said. Some of the tiger stories were finally starting to make sense now. But there was something that Thor didn't understand. How did his great-grandfather's hog rifle fit into all this? Had he used it to kill the tiger? And he guessed that Mr. Crawford must've gotten the tiger story mixed up, too.

"Of all the folklore that you've heard about Tiger," Mr. Bragg inquired, "what has been the most…unusual…or interesting?"

"The two things that most of us in this region talk about are that Tiger Whitehead was supposed to have been one of Daniel Boone's sons, and also what Tiger said on his death bed."

Mr. Bragg looked up. "Which was?"

"When everyone realized that Tiger was dying, some of his friends and relatives got together and caught a young bear cub. They took it to his house, which was up the road about half a mile, and they wanted him to kill it so he could say that he had killed one hundred bears in his lifetime."

"Really! What happened then?"

"Tiger refused to do it—even after they tried twice. He told them that he didn't get his bear that way. And for them to turn the cub loose."

"I like that," Mr. Bragg said. "'I don't get my bear that way!' Very interesting."

Thor listened carefully to every word that was exchanged between his father and Mr. Bragg. He guessed that he was part of the Tiger story, too.

"Dad," Thor said, seeing some of the men heading up the path with lights and electrical power lines. "Can we go see the camera crew?"

Uncle Tiger's Grave

"Sure, son," Thor's dad answered. "I guess they're about ready to start." Thor's dad took his hand, and they entered the woods on a wide, well-defined path. The path first crossed the rocky stream on a wooden foot bridge and then traveled almost straight up and to the right under giant sycamores and pine trees. It emerged onto a small knoll carved into the side of the forested mountain. The knoll was flat and perfectly clean, and there was just enough room for a dozen graves. Obviously, someone took care of the graveyard, because there were flowers on each well-kept grave. In the middle, the news crew was huddled around one dark stone that stood about three feet high. There were so many lights, it was like the whole world was focused in on this tiny green spot in Tennessee.

Fortunately, Thor and his dad got there a few minutes before the filming started. They had to navigate through the small crowd to find a place to stand next to a laurel thicket. Sinbad darted into the laurel leaves. From there, he could watch everything that was taking place and still keep a red-eye on Thor at the same time. Thor himself was so excited that everything couldn't happen quick enough. Then, as the camera crew and lights slowly moved in closer, the news commentator began speaking.

"Today, Channel Three is here at this mountaintop graveyard to discover one of East Tennessee's forgotten heroes. In an area that has seen the likes of Davy Crockett and Daniel Boone, lesser men often go unnoticed. One such man was James T. (Tiger) Whitehead, who is famous for killing ninety-nine bears in his lifetime. As you can see, the stones are dark and old. We're high above Tiger Creek, not far from Roan Mountain. We thought it important to bring this little-known regional history to the people of East Tennessee and western North Carolina—the people of the blue Appalachian Mountains."

It was the happiest day of Thor's young life. He had his friends, he had his family, he had the green mountains, rocky streams, laurel, and grapevines, and most importantly, he finally had his tiger!

The noted hunter

JAMES T. WHITEHEAD

BORN 1819
(killed 99 bears)

DIED
SEPT. 25, 1905

◆◆◆

"We hope he has gone to rest"

TIGER

James T. "tiger" Whitehead
was born in 1819 and grew up
when the pioneer spirit was alive
and well. East Tennesseee and
Western North Carolina, like much
of the Appalachian Mountains
during the 19th century, was a raw,
rugged land. To survive required self-
reliance, determination, and a whole-hearted
belief in the sacredness of life. From the harsh
reality of this mountain life grew a beautiful
tradition of folklore and family
that survives to this day.

Tiger Whitehead was a man of two centuries—
and perhaps two minds. He is best remembered
as the hunter who killed 99 bears
during his lifetime. Yet on his deathbed,
when someone brought him a bear cub,
he refused to kill it. Although it would have been
his 100th bear, his lifelong belief in humanity's
place within nature would not allow him
to kill it. "No," he answered that day.
"Every living wild creature has a right to its life!"

SALLIE

THE GRAVESTONE OF TIGER'S WIFE, SALLIE GARLAND
WHITEHEAD, IS JUST AS COLORFUL AS HIS. IT READS
AS FOLLOWS: "SHE WAS NOT ONLY A MOTHER
TO THE HUMAN RACE BUT TO ALL ANIMALKIND,
AS SHE GAVE NURSE TO ONE FAWN AND TWO CUBS.
SHE IS NOW RESTING FROM HER LABOR."

FOLKLORE HAS IT THAT TIGER'S WHITE-HAIRED
GHOST STILL ROAMS THE ROCKY TOP GAPS
AND CLOUDLAND VALLEYS OF THE
APPALACHIAN MOUNTAINS, SEEKING IN SPIRIT
WHAT IN LIFE HE KNEW HE HAD NO RIGHT
TO COVET—HIS 100TH BEAR!

TIGER'S AND SALLIE'S GRAVES REST
IN A BEAUTIFUL, SECLUDED SPOT
ACROSS THE SMALL STREAM KNOWN AS
TIGER CREEK, JUST BEYOND TIGER VALLEY,
NEAR ROAN MOUNTAIN, TENNESSEE.

—J. L. Küntz